T0051594

small pieces

small pieces

25 texts
25 paintings

Micheline Aharonian Marcom

Fowzia Karimi

DALKEY ARCHIVE PRESS

First edition, 2023

Library of Congress Cataloging-in-Publication Data available upon request

ISBN: 978-1-628974-50-8

Cover and interior design by Fowzia Karimi

Dalkey Archive Press
Dallas/Dublin
www.dalkeyarchive.com

Contents

The Devotional Life

An Artist's Statement

In the human body: trillions of cells, 78 organs, five senses. Though sight was neither the first nor the last to evolve, it is the pinnacle sense in my mind. The eye is the eminent organ. Next to it, the hidden organs quiver, the minor senses falter. I should build an altar to the eye!

Before language, before thought, coincident with breath, was the eye. Animated by light, inspired by form, and lusting after color, the eye. If I sweep away all thought, all memory, all noise, I am left seeing. I see, therefore I feel. I see, therefore I know. I see, and so I love. I see, so I am.

I live the devotional life. My eyes are the organ of my devotion. In the back of my eye, next to the optic nerve, sits the cardiac nerve. My eye says *What beauty! and the car diac nerve translates the message into an electroemotional one, which it carries down to my heart, where it is magnified a thousandfold and its enlargement quickens the conversation within those four chambers. At the end of my gaze is a hand that tenderly caresses a form–the bridge spanning the bay, the river's turn in the landscape, the moon's half-hidden face in the sky, the swollen orchid bud–even as my eye follows the form's contours.*

The devotional life is the tender life. What I observe, I take in. To take in is to make room. To make room is to grant acknowledgment and, in return, be gifted with acquaintance. A thing known is a thing beloved.

I first realized this when I found that through drawing and painting a grub, I'd completely fallen in love with it. In following every curve of its form with my eye, then my pencil, I became intimate with a creature I'd previously found abhorrent. In mixing my paints to match its exact colors, and while, in turns, showing or hiding the white of my paper to mimic the translucency or opacity of its skin, I fell in love with the tiny creature for everything it was. Seeing is a devotional act, so, painting, a devotional practice. I have an understanding of the grub that I did not have before I looked so tenderly at it; before I let my gaze stroke its form and my pupil drink in its colors; before I let my brush, loaded with water and pigment, glide across and release the same colors onto the paper's surface. The grub, taken in through the act of seeing, now has a room within me, its own room. And there are a million other such interior rooms occupied by millions of creatures, objects, moments, exchanges, events, places, each first observed by my eyes.

I live the devotional life. The eye is my organ of devotion. The blushing clouds at sunrise, their reflection in the window glass, the question on the woman's face, her earrings dangling, beads of honey on the kitchen counter, the insect trapped, the distance across the valley, the rock face marred, the winter light playing across my dog's fur, the angle of her cocked ear, the arc of the ball, its round imprint in the snow, the tide pools teeming, in the afternoon glow, the tiny repeating rainbows across the skin of my left arm, the unspooled ribbon, the note unread, the overlapping shadows of the houseplant's leaves on the bedroom wall, the bedsheets crumpled, the languor in his bowed frame, the book left open, on the windowsill, a teacup, the squirrel returning to its nest, the maple seed twirling, in the soil, a grub turning. I see, therefore I love.

By day, the steady stoker feeds image upon image into the imagination, keeping it lit. But at night, the eye does not rest when the lid closes over it. The eye works its second shift; flitting side to side in its socket, it projects a hundred dreams onto that curtain. I've found, over the years, that the forms that occupy space in the external world have their counterparts in the imagination. Here, they are symbols, and stand in for what is without. Often, they are a distilled representation, a more elemental rendering, of their figures in the outer world. A river in the landscape makes a dozen turns, is in places cloudy, in places limpid, in places churning; it is filled with life. A river's symbol in my imagination is a flat arcing blue ribbon. When I paint, I find I take one of two routes. I'm either drawn to paint the real-world object—the leopard shark's eye or the headstone—or I glimpse its analogue in my imagination. The first practice involves the use of the sense organ, the second the use of the inner eye, the one wired to the unconscious and, therefore, to the imaginarium.

I began painting while studying biology. I soon left my studies to become a biological illustrator. I gained greater intimacy with, and knowledge of, the natural world through closely observing and painting it. One at a time, birds, insects, plants, their feathers, mouthparts, or venation, occupied my field of vision—in a book, on the table, or through my microscope—and I fell in love again and again and again with the thing I looked at and painted. But my inner world is filled with its own images. And when reading literature, these images flash for an instant in my mind's eye. Often, they are not illustrative of the text. They are symbolic images responding to the text (because reading, another of the devotional practices, is a living/active correspondence). It's why I rarely call my paintings illustrations; to me they are illuminations. They have their own mechanisms by which they elucidate the text; they do not simply represent it. When I read, the language, imagery, and the tone of the text are consumed and travel through the imagination's alimentary system, a series of winding tubes, gearwheels, and cavernous chambers that transmute language and story into image.

Many years ago, when Micheline first approached me about this collaboration, she said she wanted her written pieces to be in conversation with my paintings. And that is, in fact, what this book is, a conversation between two artists, a reverberation between text and image. Some of her pieces excited the love I have for nature or the anguish I feel over its destruction and I found myself wanting to paint the objects of my devotion—the lobster claw, the grains in the seed bank—as they are in the world. Other pieces, or specific ideas, or language within them, solicited a symbolic response in my mind. The two execution images in Micheline's written piece produced a corresponding image in my mind: that of a libation bowl, symbolic of our long history of, thirst for, and fascination with, ritual sacrifice. Micheline's writing functions on multiple levels and has been through its own circuitous creative apparatus. It leaves open many doors, even while it is honed, precise, crystallized. Like crystal, it rings and these reverberations elicit, as answer, images in my mind. But again, I don't paint to illustrate an idea or a scene. Image has its own tongue, its own tenor, its own merit on the page. When in conversation with the text, it can illuminate. The two forms together on the page may invoke a third in the mind, a chimera, something unseen but not illusory. After all, the eye enjoys dual domain; it looks out, and looks in. It is the eminent organ, the pinnacle sense. I will build an altar to the eye!

Fowzia Karimi
February 2022

small pieces

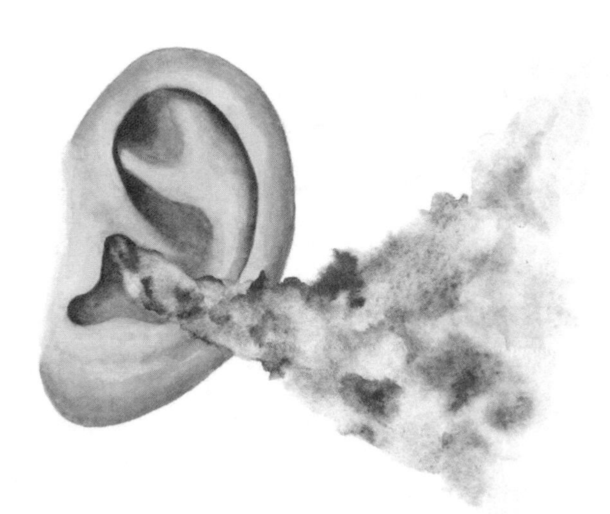

On Writing

She says:

I lean my ear in. And—

Listen.

In Winter, Again

The orange breasted robins are in the garden today for the second time this January. Dozens of them push from inside the wild berry bush near the wooden fence and fly to the top of the redwood tree and back, roiling, lifting the air as if the air were seawater and the bird movement the rise and fall of waves. Below the thrushes' wings nearer the earth the atmosphere is calm (much like the deep is unaffected by the surface's commotion) while the constant movement from bush to tree continues to make a midair ruckus—happily, it seems to her.

Last night she was fighting with her lover again and the old feelings returned again in winter. Today the new robins, their bright plumage and the morning fill with the possibilities they herald, the electric rumble they make of the invisible air, *happily* it seems to her.

Bottles (4), Hard Plastics (19), Flip-Flops (2), Plastic Bags (25), Drinking Cups (115), String Tied Up in a Nylon Sack (3.26kg)

A wide assortment of synthetic polymers weighing all together 5.9 kilograms were extracted from the sperm whale's stomach after the young male had already died in the waters near Kapota Island.

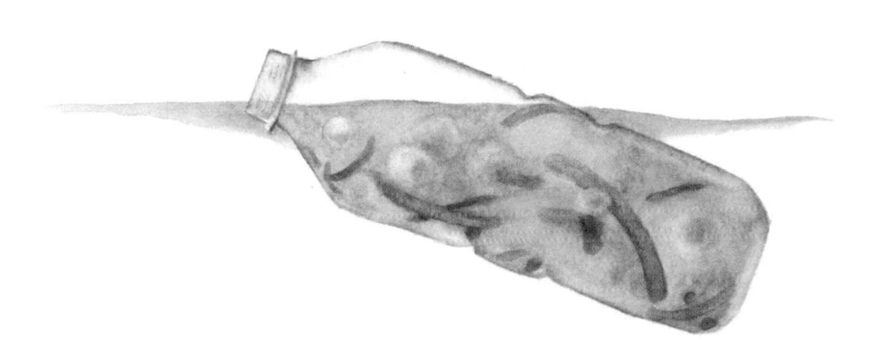

The Problem with Dogs

I walked through Oakwood Cemetery this morning between the limestone and marble headstones, past the massive branchless tree trunk on the rise with my small dog off his lead. When I noticed he was no longer trotting at my side I called out his name and spied him several feet behind me with his back leg midair readying to mark the plastic flowers of a sepulcher (my shouted protestations that he *come here now!* to no avail) and I thought to myself how little respect dogs have for the dead.

Fado November, 2009

for Fowzia

A road which was no road traversed a dry riverbed and I found bones when I traveled to the depot of bones eighty-nine years after the deportation marches from Kharpert in old Turkey to the Der Zor in Syria because I wanted to go home but the road the place did not exist, she said.

Or perhaps her life is a tether of old stories old feelings handed down one person to the next much like the lightblue cotton headscarf crocheted along its edges her great-grandmother made (she was told) for her grand-mother who gifted it to her mother and she passed it to her in a gradual move from east to west—Kharpert Beirut Los Angeles—a portable faded blue cotton estate.

Now she sits inside a large concert hall in Northern California listening to "Com Que Voz" and beneath her sternum in that small hollow (or is it a tiny convex mirror reflecting the dry riverbed, the not road, the chalky eighty-nine-year-old radius she discovered in the earth on a trip she took to Der Zor five years ago to find the evidence, she told her friend over a drink after the concert, of their existence) the old feeling returns. I know it too, her friend said: (the sea, the sunshine of Los Angeles after she emigrated from Kabul as a young girl). Because when the fadista performed the old song of separateness from the even older poem it seemed, for a moment, that everything: voice guitarra acoustic guitar; heart blood sternum and bowels; the Portuguese songs of fate; the abandoned villages and bones of the old Armenian clans in old Turkey; the newer (unrecovered) ghostly dead in Afghanistan—was brought into correspondence. Yes, her friend agreed, we can none of us ever return.

Both Beautiful and Strange

We stood in the rear garden and I noticed the sun's light begin to wane many hours before its setting in the west. My son yelled *it's time!* and we dashed to the front of the house where he held aloft a piece of cardboard he had prepared earlier at school and I lifted up a piece of white paper behind him. As the sun's light passed though the small punched-out circles on his sign L U C O emerged in crescent shapes on the paper in my hands. *Wow wow* he said.

I joined in my young son's excitement to see the fantastic shadow-letters forming his name (I kept quiet about the nervous tightening in my belly that my foreknowledge and lay person's understanding of the annular solar eclipse did nothing to allay). We continued to watch the letters transform until they and the disk of the sun were obscured.

Later back in the rear garden we observed beautiful dappled crescent shadows falling on the flagstones like snow through trees and *look, mama* he yelled in glee, half-moons cover our whole house! The shapes both beautiful and strange.

Signs

The neighbor's electric porch light shines brightly on this dark waning gibbous moon night at the edge of her small garden and illuminates a spider's web in the rhododendron bush outside her kitchen window. An orb spider moves in larger to smaller circles completing its new web and as she watches she thinks how fishing nets were once made by hand from sedges and tree fibers, how cloth was woven on simple wooden looms for millennia, and of how the forms of the letters of the alphabet originated in some measure from animal and other natural signs because all things pattern from earth, there is no outside, no separateness from it, she thinks, only the orb spider spinning its eternal (one-hundred-forty-million-year-old) web which she had not seen before tonight because usually at this hour she is sleeping (tonight the girl cannot sleep) and her neighbor has not left his porch light illuminated to reveal the dark rhododendron bush outside her kitchen window and the spider's nighttime maneuverings over the course of twenty minutes and its eventual retirement (after its labors are completed) to the center of the web where it arranged its eight legs in a star formation.

In the morning she returns to the kitchen and looks out the window and sees that the web has vanished. She surmises it was the unexpected September rain showers before dawn that destroyed it while she slept. Her neighbor later informs her that he heard thunder and saw lightning which was unusual for this part of the country.

The Leopard Shark

The fisherman pulled the leopard shark out of the salt-water bay just before three o'clock in the afternoon. The sun was shining and it felt like summer in March because it had rained almost every day for months before today. Grey skinned and black spotted. The fisherman stood at the shore near the oil refinery and the black rigs in the distance looked like black belts holding down the bottom portion of the sky. My son and I were early to an appointment with his pediatrician and so to pass a quarter hour and enjoy the warm weather I had veered off the main street where the doctor's office was located and driven three blocks to the shore near the refinery where several men were fishing and speaking to one another in Spanish. We watched as one pulled strongly on his pole for several minutes until he dragged a small shark about four feet long from the dirty bay water. The excitement of his heavy pulling on his fishing rod, including exclamations from a fellow bystander that he'd *got a big one*, kept us riveted at the water's edge. *Mira* the fisherman said and the bystander yelled *will you take a look at that* as he took the shark from the fisherman's hands and took pictures of his children posing with the hanged animal. *Lo vas a remeter* I asked the fisherman because I hoped he would put the shark back into the water and he assured me that he would because he didn't plan to eat it. The shark died on the dirty gray rocks and from where we stood its gray black spotted skin looked like leather. My son and I hurried from the scene, late now for his doctor's appointment.

As I waited in the lobby for my son I recalled a photograph I had once seen of an enormous old warehouse and inside it hundreds of thousands of otter skins piled to the rafters. The photo was taken in Sitka Alaska circa 1900 at the time the otters were slaughtered to extinction. I couldn't imagine when I saw the image that there had once been so many otters in the sea or that they had been hunted by Russian fur traders until the animals were, as a species, eradicated from Sitka Sound.

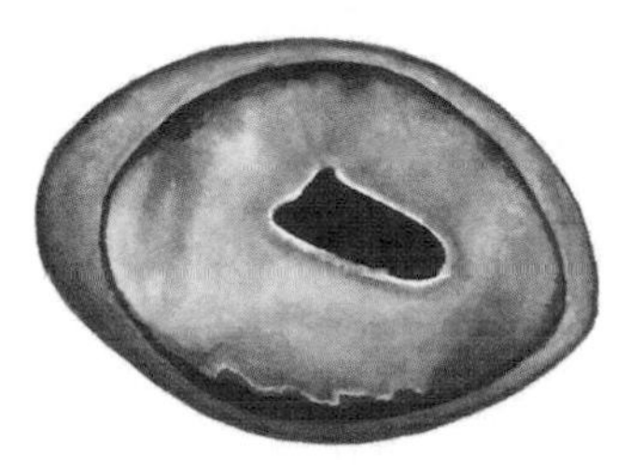

There Are So Many

Things (soaps, detergents, cleaners, conditioners, shampoos, oilstain- winestain- bloodstain- cat and dog urine-removers, plastic water bottles (in all the motley colors), frying pans, stock pots, cutting boards, chef knives, paring knives, spatulas, sponges, dust rags, dishwashing gloves, bath sheets, bath towels, floor mops, brooms, buckets, vacuum cleaners, vacuum bags, coffee makers, coffee cups, electric kettles, kettles for the stovetop, toasters, toaster ovens, hot pots, irons, gas grills, water purifiers, sparkling water makers, high speed blenders, slow cookers, indoor lights, outdoor lights, Christmas lights, six foot tall artificial trees and silver balls, red balls, green balls, tiny candies individually wrapped in gold foil, scented candles, flameless candles, hair brushes, hair combs, face cream, eye cream, skin cream, eye makeup, and more!) for sale inside the monstrous retail store in early December and they make her think of entropy and of death.

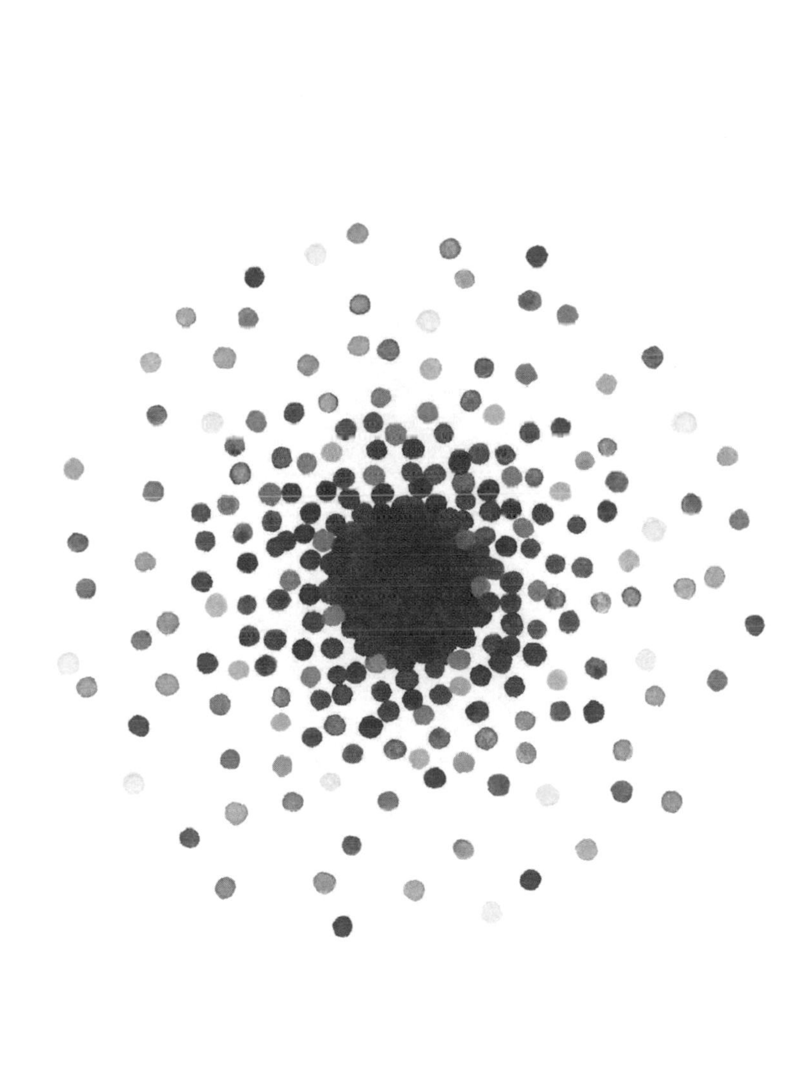

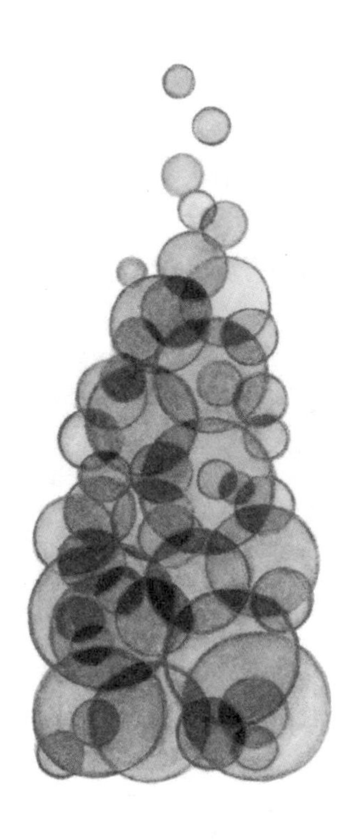

I Would Be Satisfied

If I could write (with a religious acumen) the sound water makes as it fills an empty bottle. But which words in what order to describe the increase of liquid, the attendant decreasing volume of air (the growing heft of the bottle in my hands), the variation in pitch directing me when to remove the vessel from below the spigot with ears not eyes and drink deeply?

Beauty

The last portion of the day's goldenrod light rests on the crown of the tallest redwood in the grove at dusk in mid-October. A black bird has landed there.

Taken Into Consideration

The busy bee has no time for sorrow. –William Blake

The population of the western honey bee has declined an estimated fifty percent in the United States since the 1970s and for a long time no one understood what, exactly, caused tens of billions of bees to *just disappear*.

In 2015 an independent group of twenty-nine scientists concluded that the family of petrochemicals known as neonecotinoids—a new class of neuro-active insecticides (the first one patented by the Bayer Corporation in 1985) coated onto seeds so as to be absorbed into a plant systemically as it grows—cause injury to bees and even a small, sub-lethal exposure to the poison inhibits normal cognitive function so that an affected individual can't, for example, navigate its way back home. At the time of the study neonecotinoids had become the most widely used class of insecticides in the world.

The two leading commercial manufacturers, Bayer Corporation and Syngenta Group, questioned the task force of twenty-nine independent scientists' conclusions and conducted their own in-house research to evaluate the effect of their products—Admire, Advocate, Platinum, and Cruiser—on bee colonies. The representative from Bayer Corp. said they believed the prior study was not objective, while the technical lead of Syngenta's Ecological Risk Assessment commented that while it was undeniable that if a bee is exposed to a pesticide there's stress, there are "multiple stressors and they all must be taken into consideration."

Entertainment

A man and a woman watch their children run up a basketball court inside a large gymnasium in a middle-class suburb one hour's drive from San Francisco. The woman knows the man only superficially: his son and hers have attended the same school for several years and she will sometimes see him at parent functions. She knows he is Lebanese (like her own mother) and so to pass the time as they sit on the bleachers and wait for their sons' practice game to finish she asks him about his life before he emigrated to the United States. He says I didn't come here until my early twenties so my childhood was war.

To show her sympathy and demonstrate her understanding she says that must have been terrible. (As a child she had watched the Lebanese Civil War on the news each evening in a wealthy suburb of Los Angeles.)

We got used to it, he says. When I was a teenager around the same age as our boys (their sons, meanwhile, whoop and holler with the other children as they run back and forth between the two baskets in their colorful uniforms) my friends and I would sometimes take the bus from our village to Beirut and someone, we never knew who, would hang a large white sheet on a rope at the Greenline to shield us from the sniper's view as we ran across it.

Why did you do that? she asks.

We were bored, he says.

You risked your lives for—?

During those years the only operational cinema in the country was on the other side of the Greenline, he says, and we desperately wanted to watch the latest Hollywood movie.

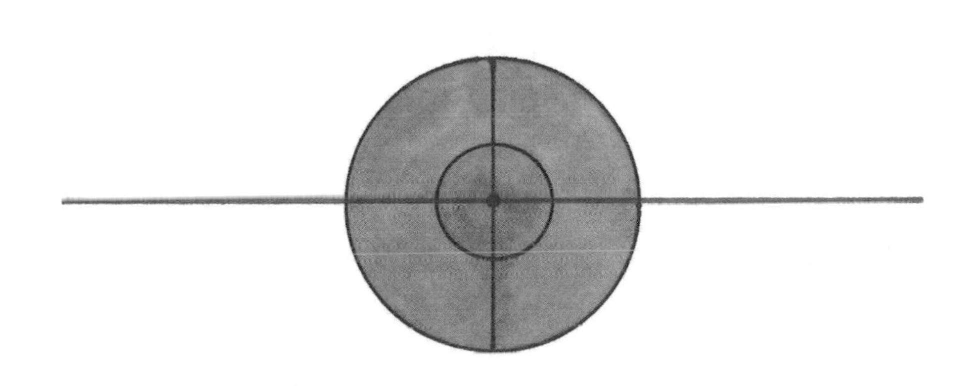

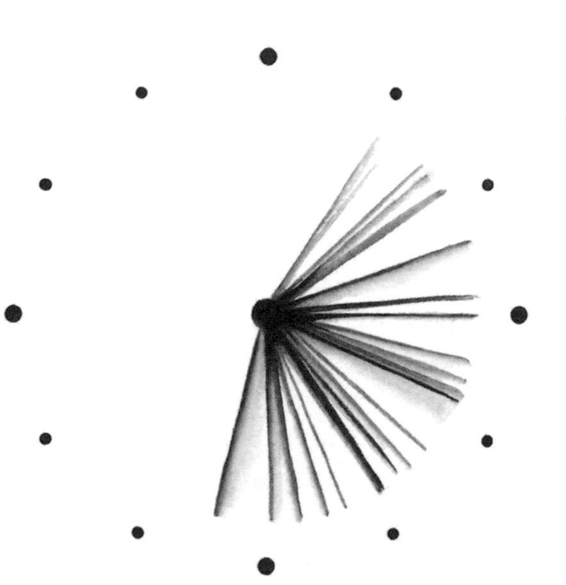

Time Apart

She sits in the red wingback chair by the large bay window, the afternoon sunlight is bent warm-yellow this time of year, and she picks up the novel lying on her lap and continues reading it. (If you were to see her in the red chair you'd notice that she looks up from her book every few minutes and at the clock hanging in the living room and then out the window again; she is counting the hours until he will stop his business of the day and drive to his home where she'll meet him for dinner at six-thirty. The day has been, it seems to her, the time apart as she waits with the abandoned novel on her lap, the angled light of the fall season diminishing through the glass, the hands on the clockface moving toward the larger numerals that will, eventually, bring them together again.)

Thus Far

The world's largest secure seed storage lies one thousand three hundred kilometers beyond the Arctic Circle on the Norwegian island of Spitsbergen. The Svalbard Global Seed Vault was built in 2008 to protect and ensure humanity's food supply in perpetuity and to operate without human involvement with failsafe protection against the challenges of natural or man-made disasters forever.

Last year in 2017 during the hottest year on record temperatures soared in the Arctic and the permafrost melted for first time flooding the opening of the tunnel of the vault. This year has been designated the *Hottest Year on Record* thus far.

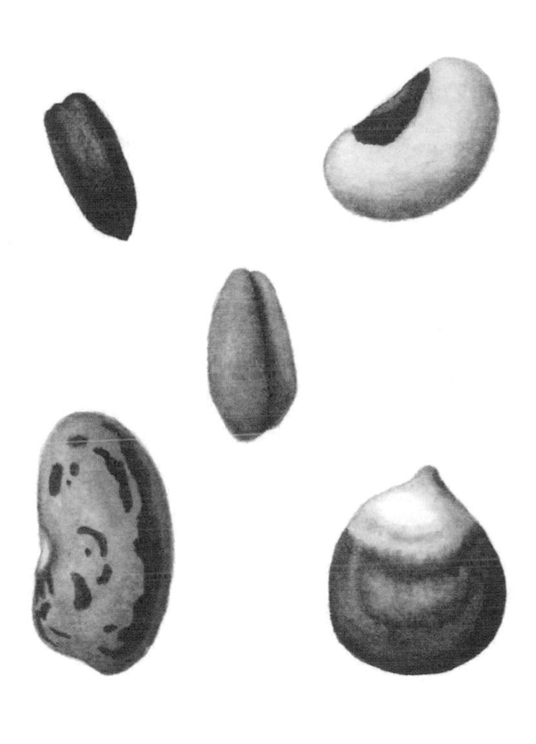

The Oracle

ΓΝΩΘΙ ΣΕΑΥΤΟΝ

She dreamed of an old god. He was a tremendous golden statue and he wore a jeweled steepled headdress like the ceremonial costume of a Thai dancer. He sat cross-legged on an altar in the corner of a room and she knew he was also an Indian deity, rotund and with the elephant's proboscis, and when he spoke he said I am Apollo, she remembers, and he conveyed his prophecies to the handsome television actor waiting before her in line and then to her. She doesn't remember his words but she recalls long before she had this vision she had inexplicably written in her notebook *you must see with the eye of the sun.*

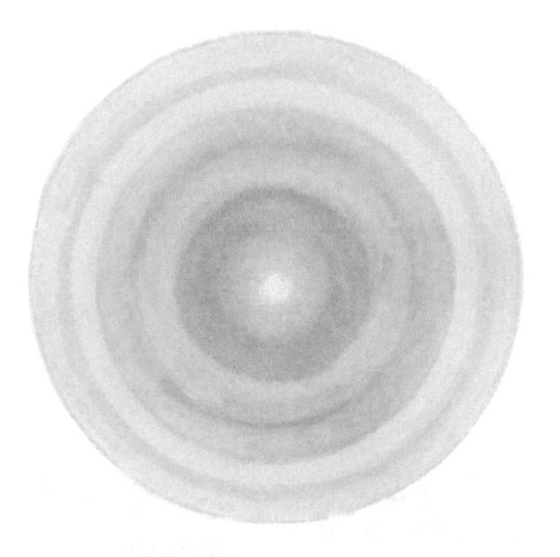

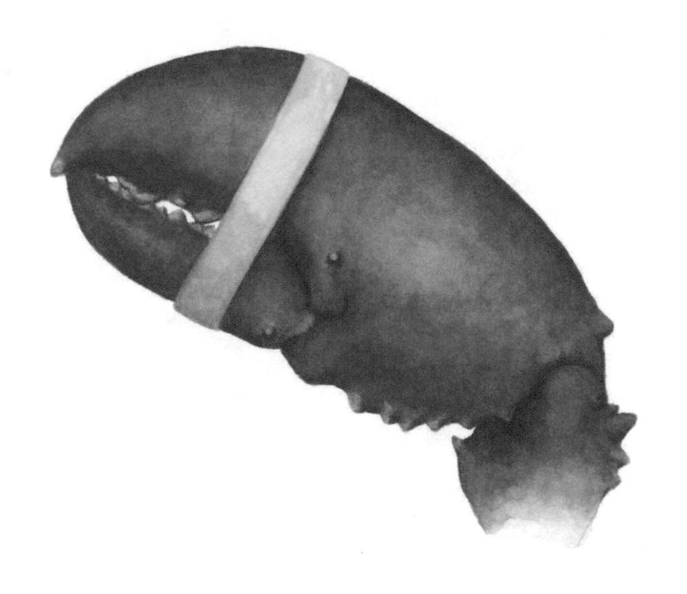

Misericordia Is a Virtue Provided It Is Not Mere Passive Sentiment or Sentimentality

The lobsters lie piled one atop the other in the aquarium at the supermarket where for $12.99 a pound you can buy a *fresh!* one for your dinner. Thick red and yellow rubber-bands clamp the crustaceans' front claws together restricting, thereby, their mobility. Those of the uppermost animal layer lurch hurly-burly across an agitated landscape while the lowest tiers of the living or dying lie mostly immobile in their own handicapped state. I stopped for a moment to admire what I might eat at some future hour and I noticed the colorful rubber-bands, the massive hobbled front claws, the strata of light-brown bodies, the jerky movement of two walkers as they pitched toward the glass

and away, each animal an unholy merchandise available
at the supermarket from 7 in the morning until 11 at night
three miles from where I live one hundred and eighty-
seven miles from the coast.

Two Things Put Together in the Imagination of the Artist Afterwards

The painting *Exécution sans jugement sous les rois maures de Grenade* by the lesser known nineteenth century artist, Henri Regnault, hangs at the Musée d'Orsay in Paris. I saw a reproduction of it by chance as I flipped through the pages of a book of the museum's collection in my home in Northern California one Sunday afternoon. The colors in the reproduction were shades of yellow, orange, red, dark green and a luminous white for a marble staircase. The tall executioner stood on the top stair in a long caftan in the style of the Moors and wiped blood from a sword in his hand with the sleeve of his robe. A man's body lay supine at his feet and in the bottom left quadrant of the canvas, two steps lower, was the man's severed head. The muscular arms of the beheaded were the most

dynamic feature in the reproduction: one lay flat with the palm facing upward in a pose of defeat, while the other was positioned at a right angle, hand pressing against the stone, as if the dead man had been lifting his torso, or his head, at the moment it was removed. Blood pooled on the white stairs between the body and head and several critics had noted the artist's greatest accomplishment was his fine rendering of it.

Months prior to looking at the glossy coffee-table book I read an article in a rock 'n roll magazine about the 'Drug War' in Mexico. Included in the feature was a color photograph of two men suspended from a bridge in Cuernavaca. The men were shirtless, their trousers had been pulled to their knees, each had blood covering his torso and thighs, and while one of the bodies faced the camera's lens, the second was turned from it. The bridge and the bodies were colored the most striking shades of orange and red in the reproduction in the American magazine, the blood appearing almost black, the second man's ass was covered by it. When I came upon the reproduction of Regnault's painting two weeks ago I remembered how one of the hanged man's arms in the photograph was positioned at a similar awkward angle and I recalled my initial bewilderment when I first glanced at it before I came to understand what I was seeing.

The documentary photograph of the two beheaded Mexicans hanged from a bridge in Cuernavaca, it seems to me now, ought to exist next to the nineteenth century painting, as they did in my imagination that Sunday afternoon, at least for the duration of the reading of these words and for no other reason than to in some small manner commemorate the dead.

In Attendance

for Luco

When the memory returns (like a specter) twenty years later it is obvious to her that *pain* is an imprecise term to describe the sensation when the energies—physical, chemical, electric, and unstoppable—surged inside her body's center and her thinking withdrew and she was without language (and the word, pain). And she recalls how she lifted her gaze to the corner of the ceiling in the living room where she labored inside that feeling she can scarcely describe even now and she saw them in attendance, some whom she recognized—her maternal and paternal grandparents—many she did not, standing in a queue shaped like a river turning this way and that in a helix of receding figures smiling at her son's passage through the cervix into the birth canal into the air and the midwife's hands who then placed him onto her chest, his dark open eyes blinking slowly in apparent astonishment at the light; and her equal astonishment, as if he'd come not from inside but from some outer realm, the pain having abated, her body an open channel in the days after she became a mother.

Old Man Eyes

I can no longer clearly apprehend the small wrinkles on my lover's face or my uneven ragged fingernails and the many imperfections I once noticed: the oil stain left by a piece of green salad I had for lunch on the collar of the blouse I wore this afternoon; a stray hair that wants plucking beneath my left brow.

Last year after my forty-sixth birthday an eye doctor diagnosed my new condition and suggested prescription lenses to correct my presbyopia. Later when I looked for the word's meaning I discovered it came from the Greek — *présbus*: OLD MAN, and *ṓps*: EYE—and I realized then I have old man eyes now.

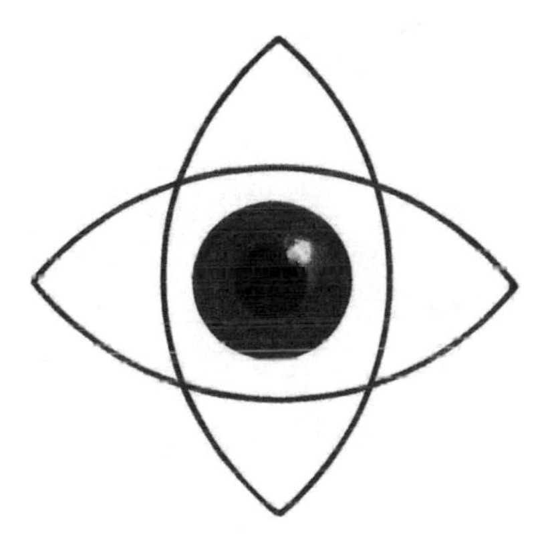

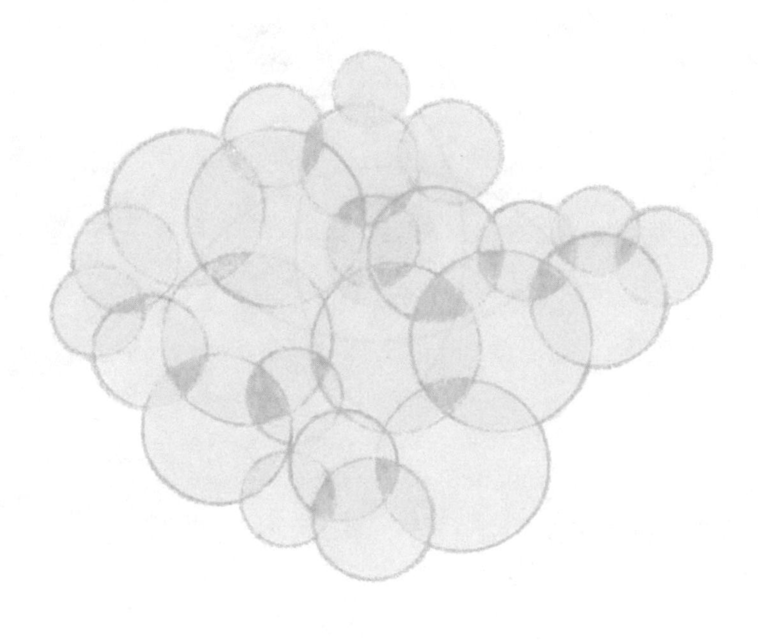

Presently

Hundreds of small yellow flowers tilt in the direction of the sun's light in a meadow adjacent to a lowland lake. She passes by them on her morning walk and she thinks about her overdue bills, a row with a colleague at work, her polluted fatty liver. The dandelion field, meanwhile, continues to press its bright yellow face toward the body of water and the sun.

At some point I won't think these thoughts any longer, she thinks, when for a moment she pauses at the lake's edge, others will crowd the mind, and at some point my mind will not be itself anymore or my pumping heart muscle, liver, its bile, the other organs, all my old thinkings. She notices the flowers turned in accord with the rays of the sun now and she imagines how at eventide the earth's shadow will cause a rupture of this natural tableau.

Upon Being Asked What Is Love

At the back of my lover's blue eye there is a blue door and when we met six years ago he said welcome and he opened it, she said.

The Miracle of Photosynthesis and Its Waste Product

She looks at the branches of the coastal live oak, inland oak, and a sequoia that all hang on the wooden muntins of the window casement and the glass like a still life in her living room. Nothing to do today, she thinks, as she exhales a loud *hhhhhaa* inside the quiet room. At the same time outside: crawling feeding insects, bird song, brown and gray squirrels, water, the mysterious transformation of sunlight, and the trees imperceptible (to her eye) change. When she now inhales her diaphragm pulls downward, her intercostal muscles lift upward, air fills her lungs and oxygen passes through air sacs into her blood. Exhaling again, carbon dioxide is rid (again) from her body.

Wallace Stevens & the News

I finish reading (*A violent order is disorder; and a great disorder is an order*) the poem and afterwards scan the news headlines on my computer. See the man in the mug shot and the cutline—*Father Kills his Sixteen-month Old Son*—because, the article reports, the son had been crying and disturbing the young father's concentration as he played a video game. How did the father do it? How did the strange order of my day proceed? First "Connoisseur of Chaos," then Reuters, then the boy's name, Daymeon.

Like this: the father was playing his Xbox at 1:00 AM and Daymeon was crying loudly so the father put his hand over the 1:00-AM-screaming-child's mouth and nose for four minutes to make the silence to focus on the game and after it ended he watched three episodes of a popular television show.

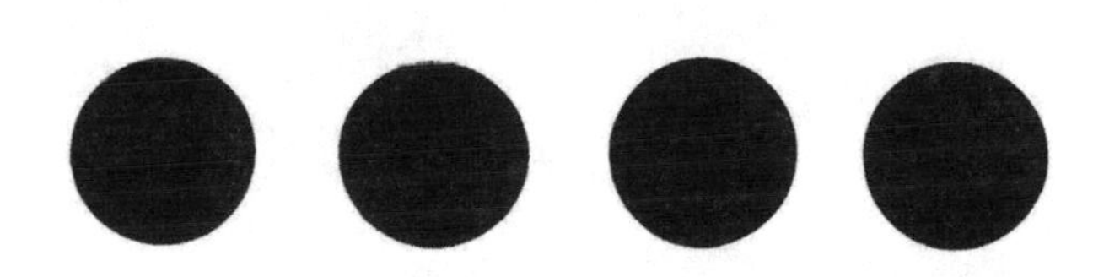

The Reader

And she has decided, or rather realized (because she has come to understand that she doesn't differentiate between these two words in her mind), that the proper way to read, to *really* read, she decides, is to hold a book in the left hand and move the eyes across the pages and letter type and into the book's far off places, while the right hand moves down into the pubic hair and tickles the pudenda and the clitoris with a loving inattention closer to home. This, she thinks, having realized it, *is* reading pleasure.

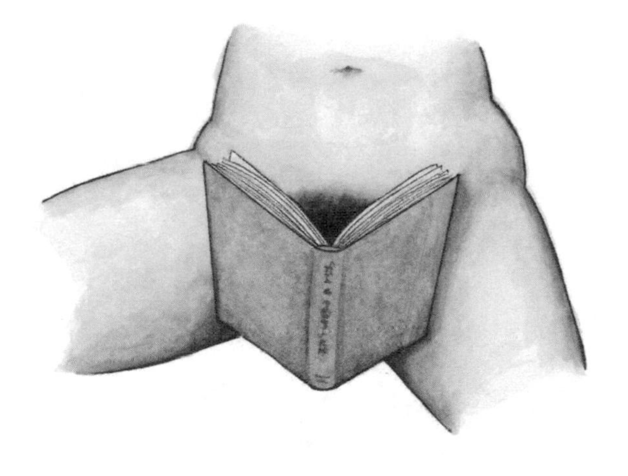

Dialogos

MM: Oscar Wilde wrote from prison "There is not a single man among those unfortunate people locked up with me who does not have a symbolic relationship to the secret of life." Can you speak to your own relationship to the secret of life, which, as Camus suggested, coincides with the secret of art.

FK: Many of us who turn to art, who devote our lives to art, do so because the practice is a revelatory one. Art unlocks the door to the secret of life. If the artist shows up with regularity, she is positioned to have a relationship with that secret, she is at the threshold of the great mysteries. Like the spinning dervish, she aligns with the mysteries regularly, rhythmically, and meaning is revealed. I am using a mystical image here because the artistic practice is a mystical one for me. But my mysticism is very much rooted in biology, evolution, and the physical universe. We live on a spinning planet that rotates to daily face the sun and revolves around the star at the center of our solar system with a precision and a regularity we feel in our bodies. We've grown our crops, fed, clothed, and sheltered ourselves in step with this clockwork. The rhythms and cycles of our universe are imprinted on our genes, as they are in all animals and plants, passed down myriad generations, and honed by evolution on this particular planet with its various potentials and limitations. We are tuned to sense alignment and misalignment in our wonderfully and terribly complex and messy lives. I practice art to realign with intrinsic knowledge; I practice art to gain an understanding of self; I practice art for the joy of it.

My relationship to the secret of life is, in fact, very much rooted in the symbolic and finds meaning through it. For me, symbology is the reduction of a thing to its essence. I write and paint to get to the truth, the essence of a thing. Metaphor in writing and form in image are rife with meaning, charged and potent, relaying and *revealing* truths. But these truths are not inscrutable ones. They are the truths of our environment and our relationship to it.

I come back again and again to time as a basic element in this relationship to symbol. The passage of time, the rhythms and flow of time inform my work. And I find I work in slow time, comparatively. The work needs time to gestate, out of the light. The symbol needs time to reduce. So art becomes an act of distillation, followed by evocation, followed by deed. Again, it is a revelatory act. This conversation you and I have been having through word and image, the work in this book, has been a long time coming. We did several of these pieces more than a decade ago. And we had many other conversations—on the page, spoken, and unspoken—over distance and time before returning to it. Suddenly, it seemed all the work was there for you. And it didn't take me long to respond to each written piece with a painting. Your work wasn't ready until it was, and when it was, it was condensed, potent, refined. What role does gestation play in your writing? And more broadly, how does the time-element function within the work, and in the process of creating it? How do you move from genesis to finished work?

MM: I am reminded of something Rainer Maria Rilke wrote in one of his *Letters to a Young Poet* where he said that *everything* is gestation and then birthing in art, and that living as an artist requires patience and humility to "wait for the hour when a new clarity is born." So time. In some ways we might say it doesn't exist: the "flow" of time, at least as we perceive it, is not real, it is in a sense a hallucination made by our minds. Calderón de la Barca put it like this: *la vida es sueño*. And what are clocks but human-invented counters that divide the cosmic turn of the earth into units? Yet time *is*, as you say, its rhythms inescapable, palpable, felt. I sometimes wonder what is time for the redwood that can live for up to two thousand years, or for a cardinal who on average lives three? There is a red cardinal outside the window on this cold winter afternoon as we await snow in Central Virginia sitting on the branch of a bush which over a month ago lost its leaves to the season. Before I could finish that sentence, the bird vanished; the bird vanished from my view that is. Then another half turn of our planet and it is now Saturday and I am back at my desk rereading your thoughts as transcribed into English several days ago in our not so very old alphabet (only 2800 years, give or take!) yet time is no thing you can see in this paragraph, writing a technology that permits the expansion and condensing of the cycles made by the spinning planets and stars for this human being who, on average in the United States, will live seventy-eight years.

And thus the reader of this collection will not know the first impulse to write the robin when I saw a nomadic flock outside the window in the back garden of my home in California (today new robins gathered in a tree in a different garden in winter, snow now on the ground on the other side of the country) or the first iteration of *In*

Winter, Again. Nor the many years of adding, adjusting the language, leaving the piece for months and sometimes years untouched, revising again, adding and changing again, thinking it was done, thinking it was not done, until finally on a particular day at a specific hour determining it was finished so that it might (and here I have condensed a decade!) presently be published. Of course "the present" might be many years from now for some readers and some readers (if we are lucky) might not yet be born! In this and other ways literature speaks from the dead. Dialogues with the future. Sometimes when I am writing I have an uncanny feeling, I sense another ineffable force at play, what Roberto Calasso described in *Literature and the Gods* as "the third actor" involved in the making of literature. "There is," he says "the hand that writes, the voice that speaks, and the god who watches over and compels." Sometimes it is as if I were a ghost already and my work already made: a strange kind of vertigo. A different level of reality accessible in the process of making books of imaginative literature, and on certain occasions while reading them. Which leads me to my next question for you: What is the proper relationship of literature to the land of the dead? How do the dead and other non-material entities express themselves in your work?

FK: I spent about ten years working on *Above Us the Milky Way*. About halfway through the process of writing the book, I had the following dream:

I was staying with my mother. She lived in the desert. Her garden was green, flourishing, but when I went out the back gate of her yard, the desert stretched out endlessly in muted grays and browns. Just behind her garden wall, a series of long clotheslines stood parallel to the horizon. Instead of clothes, large sheets of paper hung from the lines. My mother suddenly appeared behind me, having also come through the garden gate into the desert landscape. She said, "Look, Fowzia," and pointed to our left and beyond the clotheslines. I followed her outstretched arm as it traced a long line of people, faces ashen like the desert, waiting, some hidden by the hanging sheets of paper. "The dead," she said. Like silent supplicants they waited their turn. I knew they were there for me. My mother wanted to let me know. I stepped closer to one of the sheets of paper. There was writing on it, a pictographic script. It seemed to appear even as I moved in closer.

I knew early on that I would need to write about the war dead in Afghanistan—our family, friends, and neighbors who'd lost their lives to that war. And though I'd carried them within me most of my life, I couldn't write about the dead until year seven or eight in the process. Then suddenly, their voices were there, and I set down their stories one after another. I wrote. And I mourned. I grieved for the loss of their beautiful and innocent lives, cut short in brutal ways. I suffered over their suffering. I sensed them at my shoulder. I cried and mourned and wrote.

Literature is the gravesite. It is the burial hymn. It's the flower placed on the grave, the air suffused with longing and remembrance. It's where the dead go to live, where the living meet the dead. It is the gravesite but not the tomb. It's where the tree comes back to life, where the grass grows perennially. Where the heart pulses, the imagination glimmers. It is where life abides long after it has been extinguished on earth.

I know your sense of vertigo. I wonder if perhaps the writing life is not inherently a vertiginous one. The imagination demands it. It demands flight and flurry. Like you, I also sense my mortality, can trace my impermanence when I write. And when I read. I sense time expand and I sense it collapse. And while time's expansion is euphoric, its collapse is exhilarating. That I can laugh at a two-thousand-year-old joke in the pages of *The Golden Ass*, that I can experience the ecstasy of ancient ritual in Homer, morph consciousness through Ovid, mourn with

Gilgamesh or for Beowulf, find beauty in the American prairie and the American immigrant through the eyes of Cather, see myself in Woolf's mirror, that I can do all this is incredible and exhilarating. This time travel to the land of the dead, this direct communication with the spirits and spirit of earlier eras, what a beautiful and powerful thing it is. I always find it strange when people say they don't read "dead writers." What a boon the written word! The erasure of time in the pages of a book. The mirror held up, the recognition. I am and I am and I am in the pages of books. Literature is our inheritance and our bequeathal.

Never have I felt this more viscerally than when reading Whitman's "Crossing Brooklyn Ferry," a poem he directly bequeaths, and in which he directly speaks/sings, to future generations:

"Who knows, for all the distance, but I am as good as looking at you now, for all you cannot see me?

...

We understand then do we not?
What I promised without mentioning it, have you not accepted?

What the study could not teach—what the preaching could not accomplish is accomplish'd, is it not?"

I read this poem for the first time in the year after I left Brooklyn, where I'd lived on Ryerson Street, in a house only doors down from where Whitman himself had lived nearly 150 years earlier, and where he wrote "Crossing Brooklyn Ferry." Place and time were inverted; I felt it in my knees. And I sensed him at my shoulder. Yes, literature accomplishes a singular feat: it lets the dead speak to the living.

And I've felt for a long time that literature demands something of the writer in return. It asks for a sacrifice; it requires blood. Do I mean this literally? I'm not sure. It is a strong sense I have that the creative act is also a sacrificial one, that an offering must be made when a book is written. Can you speak to the relationship between art and sacrifice?

MM: Sacrifice, offerings, and blood: now we are not only in the realm of the dead, of spirit, but at the edge of the known which our minds, our beings, have long been, it seems to me, engaged with in art, philosophy, religion. I return again to Calasso who has been one of my guides inside this particular labyrinth for years: "Why should the whole world be a sacrificial laboratory?" he asks in his book *Ardor* that takes up the Vedas, "simply because," he continues "it is based—every part of it—on an exchange of energies: from outside in and from inside out. This is what happens with every breath. And likewise with eating and excreting . . . The sacrificial attitude implies that nature has meaning." Sacrifice is always addressed, he notes, to an invisible counterpart; there is destruction in this relationship *as part of this energy-exchange*, there may be a killing and the spilling of blood. Perhaps this is how and why art remains, even in secular society, a sacred domain: the invisible inextricable from it, meaning encoded in it. Some writers will still speak of the muse, much like Socrates spoke of his daimon. How might sacrifice, inextricable as you suggest from the creative act, manifest for the artist? Perhaps the end of a marriage. The death of a beloved. Exile. Loneliness. A persistent feeling of out-of-placeness; an inability to communicate deeply with many of one's neighbors, colleagues, friends, to compart one's strange, not-in-fashion thoughts and hidden feelings. Back trouble. Neck trouble. Liver on the blitz. Numbness in the hand, in the sciatic leg. Drugs, poison: the very one that Socrates took when his fellow Athenians condemned him to death. Who can say for sure? What is certain for me, however, is that writing books has been and remains the great meaningful activity of my life.

I wonder if you'd be willing to speak here of your muses and/or your daimon? How do you know you are "on the right track"? You've mentioned your dreams already, that extraordinary image of the war dead come to you: how did and do you *listen* as you write? (I know writers like other artists guard their secret process and hesitate in polite society to speak of *such* things: but are we being disingenuous in some sense if we do not?) What are your thoughts on the sacred in art? Which then leads me to questions of beauty and how, as Keats said it, it is ally to truth. What do you think?

FK: I recently turned forty-nine. And while I fully acknowledge my biological age, it fascinates me that I can look back at myself, at various ages—four, seven, twenty-eight, thirty-five—and find the same individual. Life has happened, yet so little has shifted where it matters. Of course, in some ways, I've hardened as a result of the bruising one takes as the years advance; in other ways, I've ripened/sweetened, as a result of the bruising one takes . . . But there are fundamental qualities that I was born with, that are innate, were not nurtured. It is by these inherent tendencies that I know myself. Beauty in all its forms, wherever and however it manifests—in nature, thought, culture; seen, felt, or just known— has always been my Pole Star, and has, in fact, given my life its main purpose. I write for the cause of beauty. And what would beauty be without truth to give it form? When you say there are things one doesn't speak about in polite, secular, contemporary society (and I would add, particularly in artistic circles) these are some of them: The autonomy of art; beauty as a cause; Truth with a capital T. These are not fashionable. But neither am I. I'm with the Romantics.

I grew up in a traditional and fairly religious family. Sensing this enormous *something*—Truth—I earnestly tried to find it in religion. My father had such a beautiful religious practice: personal, quiet, reverential and ritualistic. I tried to dress religion with what was innate, my love for beauty, my allegiance to truth. But at age fourteen, while deeply searching and questioning—on my own and necessarily hidden from all around me—I saw the facade crumble from the structure of religion, as it already had from the structure of society. And what was left, what had been there all along within my person, were Beauty and Truth. So the mask fell away and art replaced god.

More honesty: I've never been comfortable with the idea of the muse in the artist's life. Besides the inherent issues around gender—the fetishization of the female genii by the male artist; the effacement of her own genius by his desire (and here I depart from the Romantics)—I've never personally connected to the idea that something outside oneself might drive or engender one's creativity. This is not to say that I'm not moved by any number of external stimuli. Sometimes a single line in a book will send my head joyfully reeling. A piece of music, a bird's gesture, light across sun-drenched skin, will spark a burst of associations or responses—emotional, intellectual, corporeal. But I really believe that the source of one's art, one's creativity, is endogenous. Everything begins and ends in the self. The outer world may provide fuel, but the inner world is the machinery. The Self is the primary collector, incubator, driver, and ultimately, generator of meaning (the above Truth) and of art. We are each primed by evolution, biologically and chemically wired, nurtured and shaped by history, culture, and our daily lives in considerable and specific ways. We each have our own obsessions and patterns of being in, and relating to, the world. We each are a world unto ourselves and can draw from this deep well. All an artist requires to do her work is within her and she need look no farther than Self.

I know I'm on the right track when I am being truthful with myself, being authentic. To make art, the artist has to trust herself, trust that perhaps her art lies with her vulnerabilities—fear, loss, pain—as well as with her joys and ecstasies. To stay on track, I look to my conscious mind. Consciousness is a precious tool, a lantern that lights the way through the dim interiors of self. As much as I love and make use of my dream world and, more generally, the realm of the unconscious, I highly value the conscious mind—its hold on truth and reality; its ability to give form to the ineffable; its power to light the way through the murkier realms of self. The two components of self, the conscious and the unconscious, work remarkably well together. It is no accident.

The artist's triumvirate: Beauty, Truth, Self. Perhaps not polite or fashionable to highlight, certainly anachronistic, but art has time on its side. Our brief, small age will pass, and art will abide.

I'm speaking of beginnings. How did you first know? Was there a first work, a first experience that you can recall, which awakened you to art? It's not an easy path to take, that of a writer; much has to be left behind, given up, not once, but continually. So the draw must necessarily be a powerful one. What I'm asking is, what was your initiation? I would also love to know about the origins of this book, *Small Pieces.*

MM: Your ability to articulate so much of what I too experience in writing, the absolute requirement of trusting one's self ("every heart beats to that iron string," Emerson), as one example, the necessity of going inward, another, took me a long time to understand. Sometimes it has felt to me that the writing life is a slow, yet continual, awakening to higher levels of awareness, of consciousness, from the various mirages that pass for "reality." In terms of my initiation to writing, to answer your question, what I can say is that even as a very young child I loved *words*. I can still recall learning my letters and the exhilarating experience of discovering the hidden meanings all around me, on street signs I had passed for years, for example, so that the red octagon at the corner suddenly conveyed a message to *me* with its S T O P. Fantastic! During my childhood and adolescence, I read all the time, mostly for the magic carpet ride into story's distant realms. I read to lose my self, to become someone somewhere else: an extraordinary experience that this extraordinary technology invented by human (or divine?) ingenuity makes possible, as you've touched upon. Later, much later, hundreds of romances and adventure stories later, in my last year of high school, when I was assigned a work of literature for an advanced English course (by that time I was a fairly disengaged mediocre student who mostly read the CliffsNotes for the gist of a book) I had a strange experience when I decided to actually read part of the novel. It was something greater than an entertainment, one I would now describe as an *aesthetic shock*: a recognition on the level of soul. The book was *As I Lay Dying* and the character was Darl (who remains to this day a dear friend), he spoke to my interior self, one I had never really shared with anyone, one who until I read Darl's innermost thoughts I wasn't fully cognizant could even be spoken to in language. How to say this? Darl *knew* me, Darl was me and I was Darl and less lonely, less alienated, if only for the duration of reading. Of course I thought none of those things then, but I did learn the power and the profit of reading a difficult novel, and I had my first inkling of how certain books can create access to what I now understand as the sublime.

Many stops and starts after that: studying comparative literature at UC Berkeley; living in Madrid for a few years and studying Spanish and Latin American literature. I thought then to undertake more advanced studies and in this way spend my life reading. The formal study of literature, however, was increasingly becoming a game of imposing certain frames and political agendas, or "theories," onto books, and I finally decided against it. It is disheartening to me that in the intervening decades those ways of reading have come to predominate, so that many today who train as critics seem to have no qualms about tearing down literature's house, or trying to, in service of various agendas. This approach to imaginative literature is not only, I think, a kind of ignorance (Emerson reminded us that envy is ignorance), but a misleading, even pernicious enterprise. Misleading because it lies about literature and art and the aesthetic (from *aesthesis*, meaning "perceptiveness" in the original Greek), and pernicious because embedded in those lies is an impulse, perhaps not fully examined or acknowledged, to destroy works of art, either by discrediting them and in this way depriving new readers meaningful exposure to them, or by not introducing them to new generations of readers at all. I return again to Rilke who reminded the young poet that "works of art are of an infinite solitude, and no means of approach is so useless as criticism. Only love can touch and hold them and be fair to them." Love, the reverence for books, for the shared human inheritance that you spoke of earlier, which is so fundamental to deep reading, must, I think, always be an individual reader's foremost guide.

In my mid-twenties I finally realized that I wanted to write, and at twenty-eight I enrolled in an MFA program. There I had the great fortune to study with a teacher who not only introduced me to extraordinary books of world literature then unknown to me, but who instructed me in the age-old way of learning as an artist: apprenticeship. I continue to apprentice with books, to love them and to teach them to my students from that vantage: they remain my great teachers, dear companions in the life of mind and imagination.

But, of course, I haven't yet spoken of this book's origins! What I remember is that I first had the desire to work with the very short, the miniature, with *essences* as you would say, after about ten years of writing only long form. So the long made me curious about the short. A difficult training period ensued, by which I mean I wrote several one page "pieces" (only a few eventually made it into this book) but it took many, many years before I had the facility of compression I sought, before I could understand how to bring a piece to final form: not to over or underwrite, to honor the first inkling that brought the piece from ether onto the page while still revising and revising until each word, each phrase, the rhythms of the language, the images made in the mind, found a coherence and unity I was happy with. In some respects, I have found and still find this kind of writing more difficult than writing a novel.

As to the books that guided this project early on: Yasunari Kawabata's masterpiece, *Palm-of-the-Hand Stories*, taught me so much about the miniature in writing and inspired my earliest attempts, and Thomas Bernhard's *The Voice Imitator* showed me technique and care for the small and the pedestrian. And finally the other great teacher—the drawer—performed her duties. So, we return to time. And to this book's hour of arrival in the world. How extraordinary to have been able to share this exchange—in art over a decade as in letters these past several months—with you, dear Fowzia. Mayhap the stars aligned.

Micheline Aharonian Marcom is the author of seven novels, including a trilogy of books about the Armenian genocide and its aftermath in the twentieth century. She has received fellowships and awards from the Lannan Foundation, the Whiting Foundation, and the US Artists' Foundation.

Fowzia Karimi has a background in Writing, Visual Arts, and Biology. Her work explores the correspondence on the page between the written and the visual arts. She is a recipient of The Rona Jaffe Foundation Writers' Awards (2011). She is the author of *Above Us the Milky Way* (Deep Vellum, 2020).